Christmas Stories

Christmas Stories

Russell Punter

Illustrated by Philip Webb

Contents

The Elf and the Toymaker

December is always a busy
time of year at the North Pole.

This is the home of Santa's toy factory.

One year was especially busy. Santa's team
of tiny elves was hard at work.

Each elf had a different job.

Dennis opened the letters sent by boys and girls.

Babs checked whether they'd been bad or good.

Marco read what the good children wanted for Christmas.

Dear Santa,
Please bring me a yellow bike.
love,
Jo

Dear Santa,
I would like a doll's house.
love,
Emma X

Dear Santa,
Please can I have a new football?
love,
Ben

And Beth wrote lists of all the toys to be made.

10,674 dolls

21,832 bikes

8,979 roller skates

54,395 footballs

106,139 jigsaws

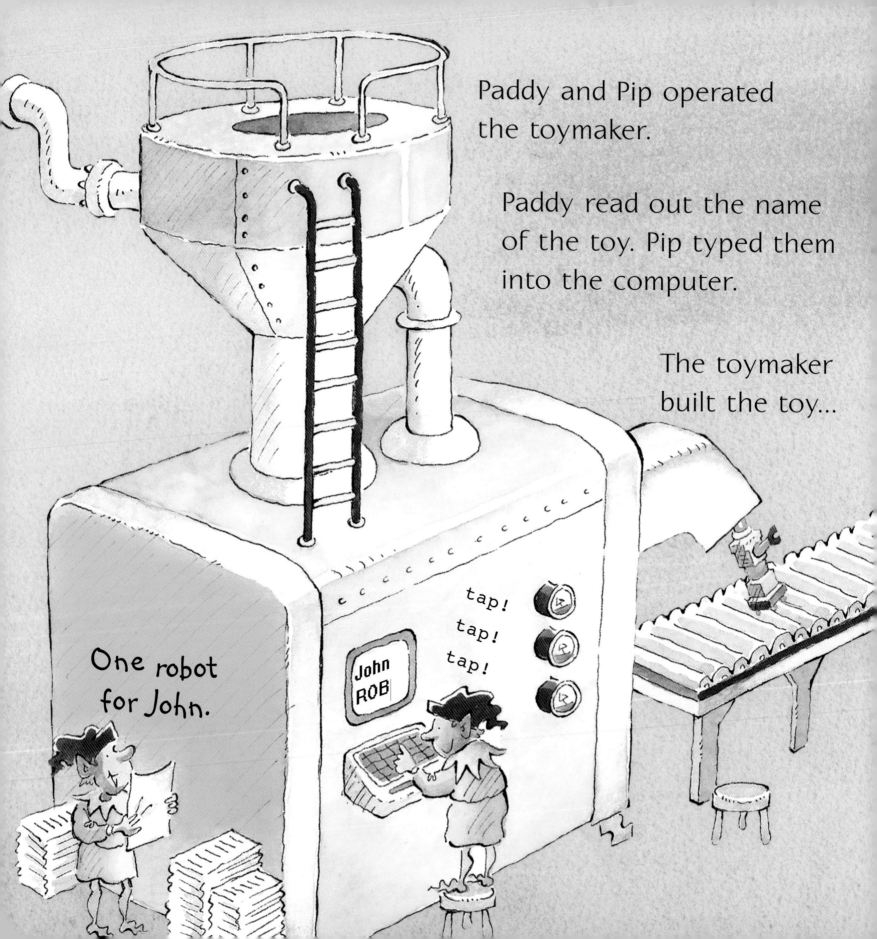

Paddy and Pip operated
the toymaker.

Paddy read out the name
of the toy. Pip typed them
into the computer.

The toymaker
built the toy...

tap!
tap!
tap!

John
ROB

One robot
for John.

wrapped it...

Splat!

and stuck on a label.

Merry Christmas to: Sam

Then Harriet took the packages to the store room.

Alfie was supposed to be sweeping the store room.
But it was so boring, he soon... fell... aslee...

"You're always asleep on the job,"
complained Santa.

"It's time to go home," he added.
"Don't come back tomorrow unless you're wide awake."

Alfie trudged off.

"If I was in charge of the toymaker,
I'd never be bored," he sighed.

Alfie suddenly decided he wanted a closer look at the amazing toymaker.

He peeked down a tube.

But he lost his balance...

and fell in!

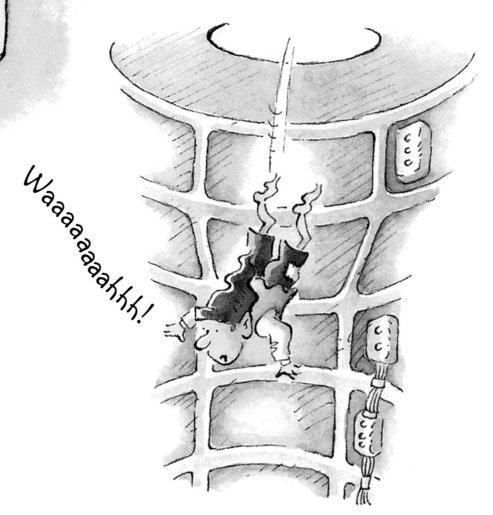

Waaaaaaahhh!

Hours later, Alfie woke up.
"I must have knocked myself out," he thought.

All of a sudden, the machine started up.

"Oh no!" gulped Alfie.
"I'll be squished to pieces."

Alfie tried to get out.

But the more he wriggled,
        the more he got tangled in the wiring.

18

But the next batch looked stranger...

and stranger...

and stranger...

until...

20

The toymaker began making
hundreds of little Alfie dolls.

Santa tried to turn it off,
but it just kept going.

The toymaker **hissed** and crunched and crackled.

Then, with an enormous burp, it shot out the real elf.

BUUURRRRP!

Wooooooah!

Santa glared at Alfie. "You've broken the toymaker."

"And there are still hundreds of toys to make."

"I'll have to give these darned dolls instead," said Santa.

So that year, instead of roller skates or footballs,
hundreds of children got Alfie dolls...

...and they were the most popular toy ever!

Next year, Santa and his elves had requests for thousands more.

The elves fixed the toymaker to make Alfie dolls and Santa put Alfie in charge...

...as long as he stayed on the outside this time.

The Fake Santa

It was the night before Christmas in Firtown.

At every home, Santa parked his sleigh...

squeezed
down
the chimney...

filled the stockings with presents...

26

nibbled the food left by the children...

Mmm, delicious.

climbed back up the chimney...

and raced on to the house next door.

Giddy up!

27

Soon, Santa was ready to visit another town.
But his reindeer were getting thirsty.

"Look! There's a river down there,"
said Santa.

The reindeers sipped the ice cold river water.

Suddenly, an angry cry came from beyond the trees.

"Hey, you. Stop!"

A snowball flew through the air
and hit Santa on the nose.

"Ouch!" he cried.

A crowd of people stomped up to Santa.

"You upset my children!" yelled a woman.

"You ought to be locked up!" shrieked another.

"What are they talking about?" whispered Rudolph.

"I've no idea," said Santa.

"Get him!" bellowed a man.
Snowball after snowball pelted Santa.

He jumped into his sleigh.

Let's get out of here!

Santa's reindeer carried him away to safety.

"I can't understand it," said Santa.
"People usually like me."

"Something strange is going on," said Santa.

"Look down there,"
Rudolph called excitedly.

34

"Hey. It's a sleigh just like ours," said Dancer.

Santa decided to fly down
and take a closer look..

The other sleigh was old and tattered.
The 'reindeer' tied to it was a
horse with antlers strapped on.

Santa followed a trail of footprints inside.

There stood... another Santa!
Two children sat sadly by a Christmas tree.

"I made a mistake, kids," growled the other Santa.

"You've been naughty,
so I'm taking back all your presents."

Drop that sack,
you thief!

"Rats!" snapped the man, seeing the real Santa.
He grabbed his sack and rushed out.

The crook leapt into his sleigh full of stolen presents and raced away.

Santa chased him into town.

The thief jumped off his sleigh and ran down a narrow alley.

The tall crook sprang over
a high wall.

I'll fix you!

Santa flew his sleigh over the wall
and hovered above the crook.

"Hey, you!" he cried.

The crook looked up and Santa emptied his sack. The fake Santa was squashed by a shower of presents.

Santa took the thief back to the houses he'd robbed.

At each one, the fake Santa
gave back the stolen presents.

Hooray for
the real Santa!

Then Santa made his last delivery in Firtown...

...to the local police.

Bah!

42

Santa's Day Off

Of all the days of the year,
Santa likes December 26th best.

It's his day off.

After one tiring Christmas,
Santa was ready to put his feet up in front of the fire.

Santa snuggled into his armchair
and put a slice of Christmas cake by his side.

He was just about to take
a sip of hot chocolate when...

...two elves burst in.

"We can't get into our house," wailed Paddy.

We need your help.

"There's a huge polar bear blocking the way," cried Pip.

Santa followed the elves to their home.
A fierce polar bear was pacing up and down outside.

"Food would tempt her away," said Santa.

"If only we could reach the sausages in our kitchen," said Pip.

Santa had an idea.

He climbed up to the chimney...

...and squeezed inside.

Seconds later, Santa came out carrying a polar bear cub.

"It must have climbed in
through an open window," cried Pip.

"That's why the mother bear wouldn't let you in," said Santa.

"She was protecting her cub."

The two bears plodded away happily.

Thank you, Santa.

"Now I can get back to my cake," said Santa.

Santa had just settled back in his armchair, when Marco rushed in.

"Calm down, Marco," said Santa.
"Now, what's the matter?"

"We accidentally left someone off
this year's list," cried the elf.

Look!

Elf delivery note

Name: Jason Jeffries

Place: Australia

Would like: A bicycle

Sign below when item
has been delivered:

"Bring me a bike from the store room,"
sighed Santa. "I'll get my sleigh ready."

An hour later, Santa landed at Jason's house.

As Santa approached, he heard voices.

"Perhaps you'll get your red bike next year, Jason," said a man.

Santa looked down at the bike. It was blue.

He took a deep breath and returned to his sleigh.

One return trip to the North Pole later,
Santa was back – with a red bike.

Jason was overjoyed.

Santa headed north again.

He was almost home, when he heard a cry for help.

Santa went to investigate.

A farmer was standing by a frozen lake.

"My sheep have wandered onto the ice, Santa," he said. "And it's starting to crack."

Please don't let them drown.

Santa flew his sleigh just above the sheep.
"Hover here, boys!" he cried to his reindeer.

Easy does it,
Santa!

Baa!

Baa!

One by one,
Santa bundled the sheep into his sleigh.

The ice cracked just as Santa
lifted up the last one.

Santa returned the sheep to the grateful farmer.

One flock, safe
and sound.

Thank you,
Santa!

Santa was exhausted.

When he got home,
he staggered into his living room.

"My hot chocolate will be cold by now," sighed Santa.
"And I bet that cake is as dry as dust."

But he was in for a surprise.

How?

By his armchair was a mug of steaming hot chocolate,

a pile of cakes

and a stack of storybooks.

Even Santa's slippers were warming
by the newly lit fire.

Suddenly, elves flooded into the room.

Welcome home,
Santa.

"How kind of you all," smiled Santa.

"Our pleasure," said Paddy. "You've shown us
that kindness is what Christmas is all about."

Chilly
and the
Bonfire

Jack pulled back his bedroom curtains.
Fresh snow covered the ground outside.

Pulling on warm clothes,
Jack ran out into the crunchy snow.

"I'm going to build the best snowman ever," he thought.

First he made the body and the head...

added two black pebbles for eyes...

four more for a smiley mouth...

stuck in a carrot for a nose...

and finished off with a hat and scarf.

Jack stood back to admire his new snowman.

"I'll call you Chilly," he said proudly.

Jack heard banging from the field next door.

Mr. Oats was putting up a sign.

Jack licked his lips. He loved marshmallows.
"Can I come to your party, please?" he asked the farmer.

"Of course, Jack," replied Mr. Oats.

"I'll let you in for free if you help me build the bonfire."

Soon, Jack and Mr. Oats had built a huge bonfire.

But, the next morning, it had vanished.
New footprints led from Jack's house
to where the bonfire had been.

"What have you done with my bonfire?"
shouted Mr. Oats.

"It wasn't me," sniffed Jack.

"I don't like people playing tricks on me," said the farmer. "You're banned from the party."

Jack felt terrible.

Mr. Oats built a new bonfire and stomped home.

That night, Jack couldn't get to sleep.
"Who would steal a bonfire?" he asked himself.

Just then, he heard the clattering of wood
outside. Jack raced out of the house.

He was amazed by what he saw. Chilly
the snowman was taking down the bonfire.

"Oh no," cried the snowman.
"We're not supposed to let
people see us move."

68

"You're alive!" gasped Jack.

"Of course," said Chilly. "All snowmen come alive at night."

Grand Christmas Party

Oats' Farm - Saturday Dec 24th 6:00pm

Music, Dancing, Games,
Hot Chocolate, Toasted Marshmallows,
Blazing Bo...

Buy your tickets at...

"So *you* took my bonfire?" said Jack.

"Yes," said Chilly, looking ashamed.

"But why?" asked Jack.

"It was so close, I would have melted,"
explained Chilly. "I didn't want that to happen.
You made me so well."

"I didn't mean to get you into trouble,"
added Chilly sadly.

"Don't worry," said Jack.
"All we have to do is move the fire."

The pair spent all night building a new bonfire on the other side of the field.

Chilly returned to his place just before Mr. Oats arrived.

"I've built you an even bigger bonfire, Mr. Oats," said Jack. "And I think it looks much better over here."

Mr. Oats was so impressed,
he let Jack go to the party.

And only Jack noticed the snowman
next door give him a grateful wink.

72

Snowy and Icy

The children of Frostly were hard at work.
Tomorrow was judging day of the
Best Snowman Contest.

Emma Humble was finishing her snowman, Snowy.

He had a battered felt hat...

tiny stones for his eyes and mouth...

a moth-eaten woolly scarf...

and a broken old walking stick.

Rich Daphne Dosh lived next door.
She had servants to build her snowman.

They called him Icy.

He had a shiny top hat...

sparkly buttons for
his eyes and mouth...

a spotted silk scarf...

and a silver-topped cane.

Daphne peered over the fence at Emma.

"Icy is twice as nice as your snowman," she boasted.

"At least I built Snowy myself," said Emma.

That night, the snowmen of Frostly came to life.

Icy pointed at Snowy. "What a frightful sight," he laughed.

Snowy looked at his tattered clothes with his stony eyes. "You'll never win the contest," said Icy smugly.

"Maybe I can make myself look better," said Snowy.

He set off across the fields.

Icy was certain he'd be the best snowman in town. But he decided to follow Snowy just to make sure.

Snowy saw sheep's wool caught on a fence.

"I could use that to patch up my scarf," he thought.

Icy crept up behind Snowy.

"We'll see how your scarf looks after it's been tangled in that wire," he chortled to himself.

Icy was about to push Snowy into the fence
when he heard a loud 'Baaaa!'
A flock of sheep raced by and knocked him down.

Snowy walked on to the woods.

"That long branch would make a great walking stick," he said.

Icy climbed a tree behind Snowy.

"I'll get you this time, stony face," thought Icy.

Icy began sawing through a heavy branch.
"This will put a dent in Snowy's hat,"
he chuckled.

But the silly snowman had cut through
the branch he was sitting on...

Icy fell out of the tree
and landed in a prickly holly bush.

Snowy tucked his new stick
under his arm and walked on.

Snowy came to
an icy pond.

Lots of shiny round
pebbles lay around
the edge.

"These will make great buttons," thought Snowy.

Icy tip-toed up behind him.

Just as Icy went to push Snowy
into the pond, Snowy bent over.

85

Icy flew over Snowy, slid silently across the ice
and vanished into a patch of reeds.

Snowy put on
his new buttons
and plodded back to
Emma's house.

Snowy admired his new stick and buttons,
then he mended his scarf.

When Icy staggered home, he looked a mess.
He was covered in leaves and reeds.

The next day, the snowmen were judged.

Scruffy Icy came last and Snowy won first prize.
Daphne was furious.

Emma was thrilled.

But she never found out
how her snowman got his new outfit.

Freezy's New Buttons

Freezy gave a sad sigh.
Every snowman in town had
shiny pebble buttons, except for him.

Crispy had three
big buttons...

Sneezy had four
small ones...

and Shiver had
eight of all sizes.

That afternoon, two men rushed
along Freezy's street.

"Where can we hide 'em, Stan?"
panted one.

"I've got an idea, Lenny,"
gasped the other.

He pulled a little bag from his pocket.

Stan took three shiny stones from the bag
and stuck them in Freezy's chest.

"Buttons!" laughed Lenny.

"Let's get out of here," said Stan.
And the sneaky pair ran off.

Freezy was dying to show off his new buttons.
But he had to wait until night time.

As soon as it got dark, Freezy visited his friends.

"What do you think of my buttons?"
he said with a grin.

"Wow! They're so sparkly," gasped Crispy.

"Better than pebbles!" cried Sneezy.

"Where did you get them?" asked Shiver.

"Oh, they were a present," said Freezy proudly.
His friends were so jealous, their snow nearly
turned green.

As Freezy strolled home,
            a newspaper blew around his feet.

The newspaper headline nearly melted Freezy with shock.

The EVENING BLAB

JEWEL THIEVES STEAL DIGBY DIAMONDS

Stan Snatch

Crooks get away with three jewels worth 1 million from Christmas display

The diamonds

Lenny Grab

Freezy was wearing stolen jewels. "I'd better hand them in to the police," he thought.

At that moment, he heard a familiar voice behind him. "There he is, Lenny!" The two crooks raced up to him.

To the thieves' amazement, Freezy ran off in fright.

"He's alive?" screamed Lenny.
"After him!" yelled Stan.

The crooks chased Freezy up into the hills.

Freezy stopped to catch his breath. He was exhausted. "They're bound to catch me soon," he puffed.

Then he had an idea.

When the crooks caught up with Freezy,
they found him sitting under a ledge.

"He's taken the jewels off his chest," said Lenny.

"Hand 'em over, snow features!" barked Stan.

"I'm sorry," said Freezy. "I can't hear you."

"Where are the diamonds?" yelled Lenny.

"Excuse me?" said Freezy.
"Where are the jewels?" roared Stan.
"Speak up," said Freezy.

The crooks' shouting made
the snow on the hillside shake.

With an huge whoosh,
it thundered down.

Freezy took the diamonds from under
his hat and stuck them in the snow.

He pulled Stan's phone from his pocket
and called the police.

He told them where to find the crooks and the jewels.

Then Freezy ran off so the police wouldn't see him.

But perhaps they did...

The next day, a policeman pinned a
shiny silver medal to Freezy's scarf.

That was even better than a button.

Edited by Lesley Sims and Jenny Tyler

First published in 2007 by Usborne Publishing Ltd., Usborne House,
83-85 Saffron Hill, London EC1N 8RT, England. www.usborne.com
Copyright © 2007 Usborne Publishing Ltd.